HOT DAY ON ABBOTT AVENUE

by **Karen English**

Illustrated by
Javaka Steptoe

Houghton Mifflin Harcourt
Boston   New York

Originally published in hardcover in the United States by Clarion Books, an imprint of Houghton Mifflin Harcourt
Publishing Company, 2004. • For information about permission to reproduce selections from this book, write to
trade.permissions@hmhco.com or to Permissions, Houghton Mifflin Harcourt Publishing Company, 3 Park Avenue,
19th Floor, New York, New York 10016. • hmhbooks.com • The illustrations were executed in cut paper and found-ob-
ject collage. The text was set in Shannon Bold. • All rights reserved. • Library of Congress Cataloging-in-Publication
Data • English, Karen. Hot day on Abbott Avenue / by Karen English : illustrated by Javaka Steptoe. p. cm.
Summary: After having a fight, two friends spend the day ignoring each other, until the lure of a game of jump
rope helps them to forget about being mad. ISBN: 0-395-98527-7 [1. Best friends—Fiction. 2. Friendship—Fiction. 3.
Rope skipping—Fiction. 4. African Americans—Fiction. 5. Summer—Fiction.] I. Steptoe, Javaka, 1971– ill. II. Title. PZ7.
E7232 Ho 2003 [E]—dc21 2002009043 ISBN: 978-0-395-98527-4 hardcover • ISBN: 978-1-328-50006-9 paperback •
Manufactured in Malaysia • TWP 10 9 8 7 6 5 4 3 2 1 • 4500750789

For Niangi, T'Andra, Maisah, Ameera, Asmani, and Sara
—K.E.
Dedicated to everyday magic
—J.S.

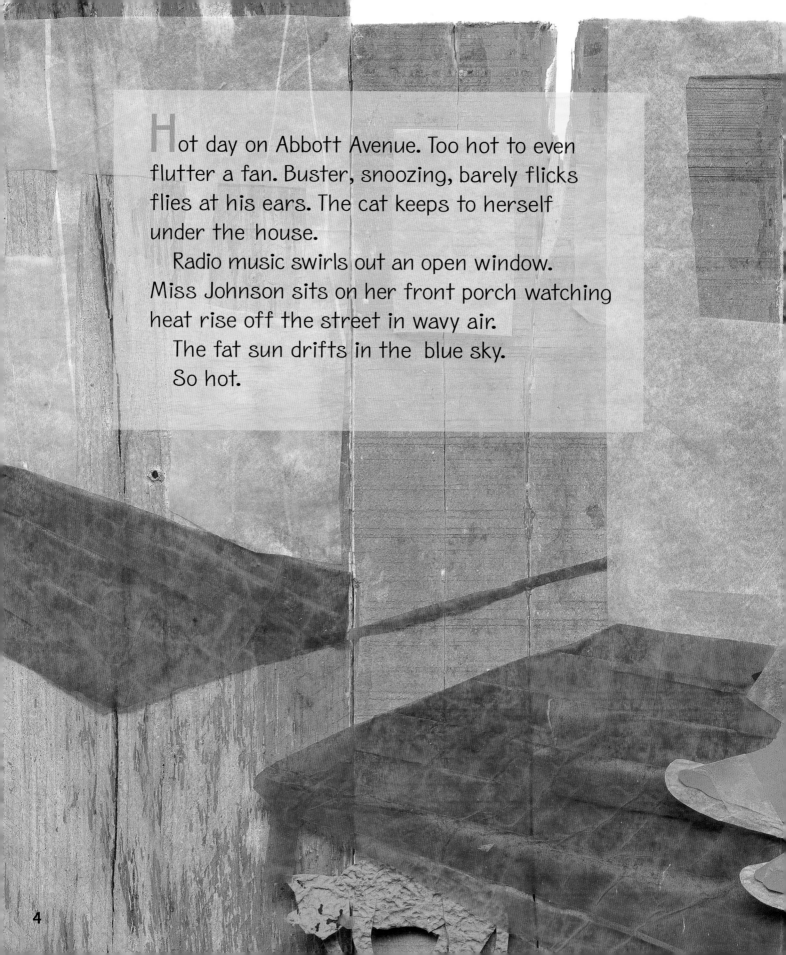

Hot day on Abbott Avenue. Too hot to even flutter a fan. Buster, snoozing, barely flicks flies at his ears. The cat keeps to herself under the house.

Radio music swirls out an open window. Miss Johnson sits on her front porch watching heat rise off the street in wavy air.

The fat sun drifts in the blue sky.

So hot.

Renée sits in the grass looking for four-leaf clovers. She finds not a one. She sneaks a peek at Kishi.

Kishi sits on her front porch counting mosquito bites. She counts seven. She sneaks a peek at Renée.

"Hey," Miss Johnson calls out.
"You girls still mad?"
"Forever!" Kishi answers.
"Forever and a day!" Renée adds.
It's a best-friend-breakup day.

Later, when the fat sun drifts toward the tall stand of pine, Kishi sits on her front porch doing nothing at all. Renée sits on her front porch doing the same.

"Come on over here and help me with my crossword puzzle," Miss Johnson says. "You know how long it takes me when I don't have you-all's help."

"No thanks," Kishi says.

"Not today," says Renee.

Not on a never-going-to-be-friends-again day.

Later still, when the fat sun kisses the tops of the trees, Kishi aims the water hose straight up, then jumps through the waterfall. So cool.
Renée plays hopscotch by herself.

"You girls want to help me weed?" Mr. Paul asks, kneeling in his flower bed.

"Not today," Kishi says.

"No thanks," says Renée.

No working together on a never-speak-to-her-again-even-if-she-was-the-last-person-on-earth day.

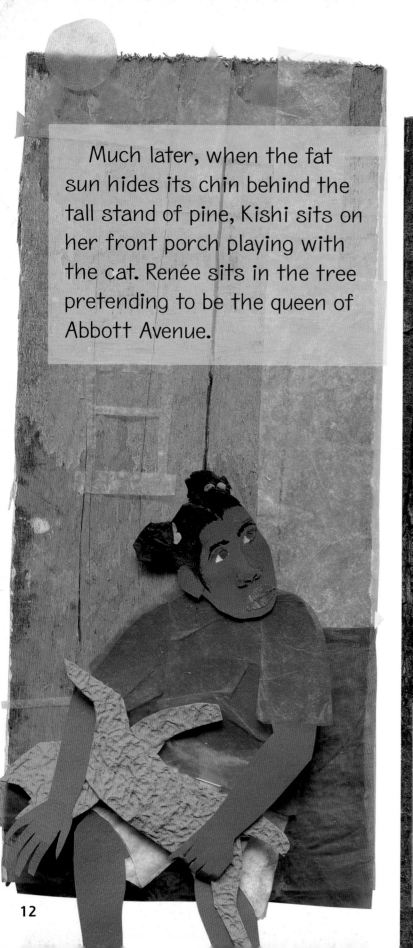

Much later, when the fat sun hides its chin behind the tall stand of pine, Kishi sits on her front porch playing with the cat. Renée sits in the tree pretending to be the queen of Abbott Avenue.

"Come on and help me make a pitcher of ice-cold lemonade," Miss Johnson says, coming out of her house holding a wooden spoon. "It's too hot to stay mad."

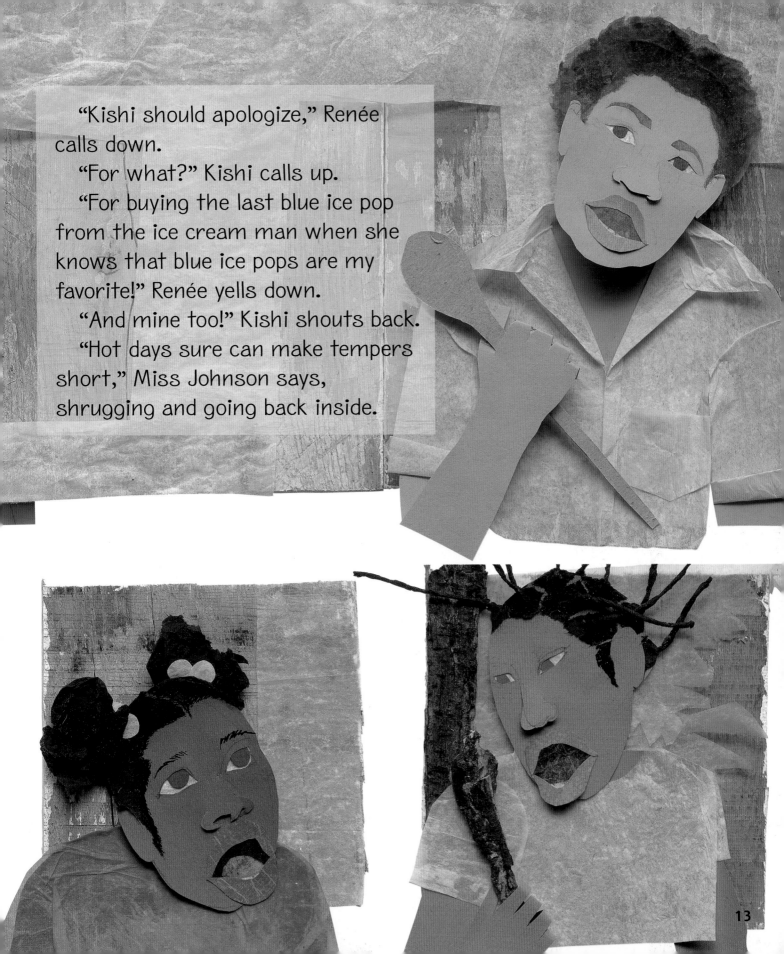

"Kishi should apologize," Renée calls down.

"For what?" Kishi calls up.

"For buying the last blue ice pop from the ice cream man when she knows that blue ice pops are my favorite!" Renée yells down.

"And mine too!" Kishi shouts back.

"Hot days sure can make tempers short," Miss Johnson says, shrugging and going back inside.

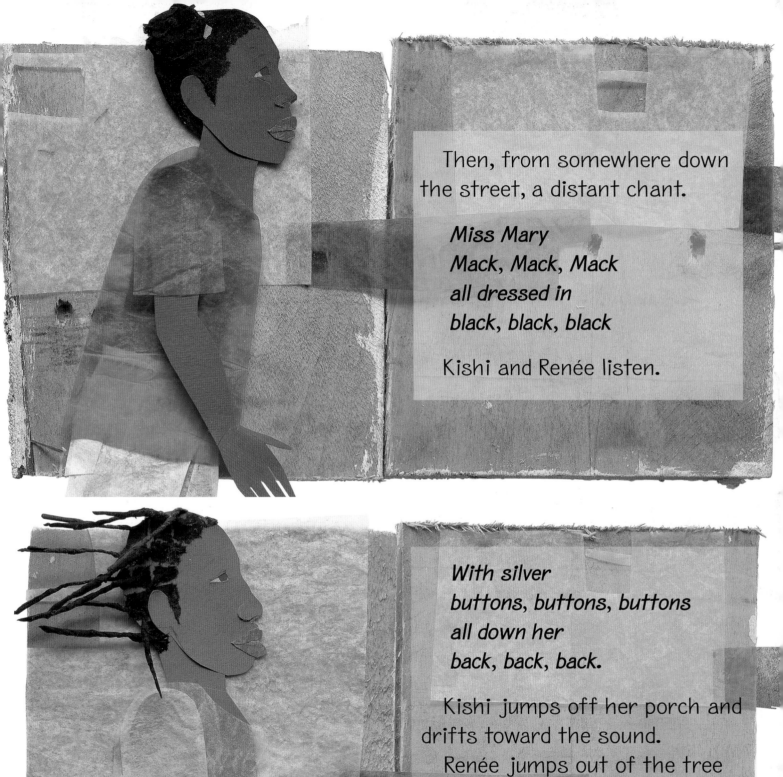

Then, from somewhere down
the street, a distant chant.

Miss Mary
Mack, Mack, Mack
all dressed in
black, black, black

Kishi and Renée listen.

With silver
buttons, buttons, buttons
all down her
back, back, back.

Kishi jumps off her porch and
drifts toward the sound.
Renée jumps out of the tree
and drifts toward the sound.

15

She asked her mother, mother, mother
for fifty cents, cents, cents

It's Darlene and Aja and Nicky.

To see the elephant, elephant, elephant
jump over the fence, fence, fence.

Jumping double dutch!

Kishi begins to run. Renée too.
Down Abbott Avenue to the
chanting sounds and the
humming ropes.

*It jumped so high, high, high
it touched the sky, sky, sky . . .*

Now it's a jump day!
A jump-in-lucky-socks day!

"Take my end," Darlene orders, and Renée runs to take the rhythm out of Darlene's hands.

"Take mine," Aja says, and Kishi runs to do the same.

Now it's a ropes-hitting-ground day! A ropes-making-a-rainbow day! Ropes swishing air, whistling air, strumming air, kissing air.

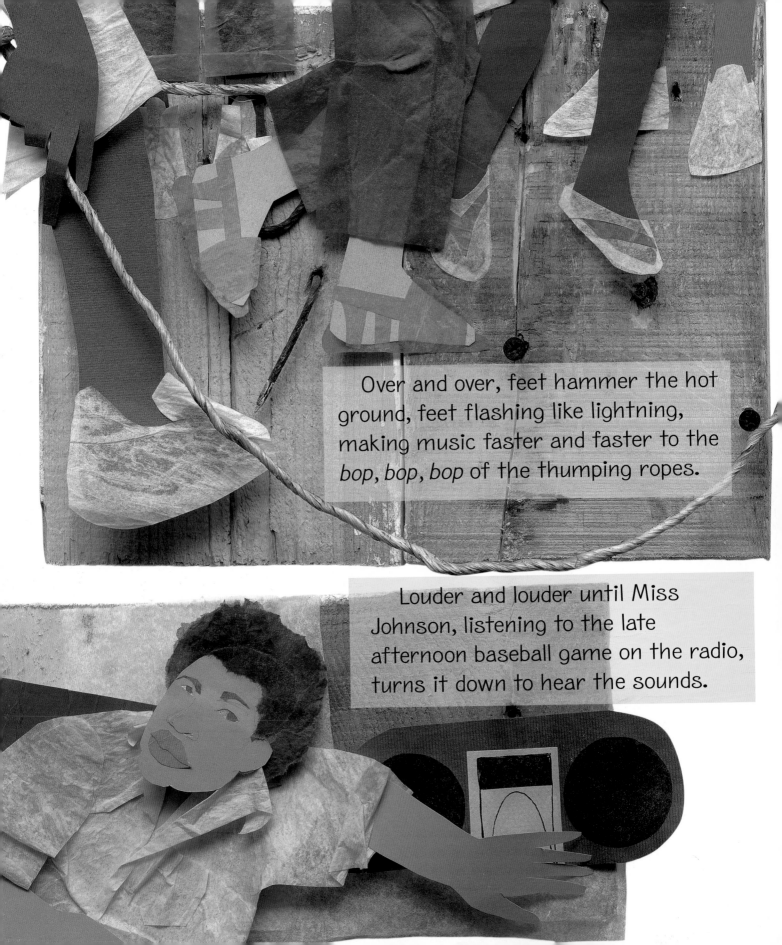

Over and over, feet hammer the hot ground, feet flashing like lightning, making music faster and faster to the *bop, bop, bop* of the thumping ropes.

Louder and louder until Miss Johnson, listening to the late afternoon baseball game on the radio, turns it down to hear the sounds.

In came the doctor, in came the nurse, in came the lady with the alligator purse!

21

Mr. Solomon, the mailman, coming down the street, stops to listen.

Mrs. Foster, sweeping the walk at the corner grocery, does the same.

Even Buster stops his afternoon snooze, looks up, ears forward, then flops back down.

The cat slithers out from under the house, takes a long look, then tips on down the street.

All of a sudden, Kishi hears something. It sounds like the tinkle of the ice cream truck. Again! Twice on this hot, hot day. She slows the ropes. Heads turn. Ropes fall to the ground.

Down the street they race for blue ice pops. So good!

Darlene buys a blue ice pop.
Aja does too. Blue ice pop for Nicky,
and one for Kishi. But none for Renée.
They're all gone.

"Here, Renée, you can have half of mine,"
Kishi says, breaking hers in two.
"Thanks, Kishi," Renée says, smiling shyly.
"You're welcome," Kishi says, smiling back.

The fat sun has slipped completely behind the tall stand of pine. The girls sit on Renée's porch slurping blue ice pops and watching Buster chase the cat back under the house, watching Miss Johnson sleep with her head back, watching Mr. Paul trim his hedges.

Pale blue juice drips down their arms—all the way down to their elbows.

"Look what I can do," Renée says, trying to lick blue ice pop juice off her elbow. Kishi laughs and tries to do the same.

Then it's a trying-to-lick-blue-ice-pop-juice-off-your-elbow day.

A forgetting-all-about-what-you-were-mad-about day.

A feeling-good-about-being-best-friends-again day.